Presented by

Tom and Michele Eroh,
Ken and Marty Hackett,
Peggy Ellen Scheridan

In Memory of

David Rees

Brand-new Pencils, Brand-new Books

Diane deGroat

HARPERCOLLINS*PUBLISHERS*

Brand-new Pencils, Brand-new Books
 For information address HarperCollins Children's Books, a division of HarperCollins Publishers, 10 East 53rd Street, New York, NY 10022.
www.harpercollinschildrens.com

Library of Congress Cataloging-in-Publication Data
De Groat, Diane.
Brand-new pencils, brand-new books / Diane De Groat.— 1st ed.
p. cm.
Summary: Gilbert's excitement over starting first grade turns to worry that the teacher will be mean, the work too hard, and his classmates too unfriendly, but throughout the day there are pleasant surprises.
ISBN-10: 0-06-072613-X (trade bdg.) — ISBN-13: 978-0-06-072613-3 (trade bdg.)
ISBN-10: 0-06-072615-6 (lib. bdg.) — ISBN-13: 978-0-06-072615-7 (lib. bdg.)
ISBN-10: 0-06-072616-4 (pbk.) — ISBN-13: 978-0-06-072616-4 (pbk.)
[1. First day of school—Fiction. 2. Schools—Fiction.] I. Title.
PZ7.D3639Br 2005 2004004179
[E]—dc22

Typography by Al Cetta ❖ First Edition
09 10 11 12 13 LPR 10 9 8 7 6 5 4

To all the Mrs. Byrds out there, especially Ann Shea

“Tomorrow’s the first day of school,” Father said. “Do you have everything ready?”

“I do,” said Gilbert.

“I do, too,” said Lola. “I’m going to school with Gilbert!”

Gilbert frowned. “No, Lola,” he said. “I’m going to big kids’ school. You’re going to preschool.”

At bedtime, Gilbert checked his new backpack. Inside were his brand-new pencils and his brand-new notebooks. He was excited about being in first grade.

Lola had a new backpack, too. Inside was her stuffed rabbit. Lola wasn't excited.

Gilbert said, "Preschool is fun, Lola. Mrs. Duck is nice."

Lola sighed. "I'll go," she said, "but I won't like it."

The next morning, Gilbert walked to school with Patti and her mother.

"I hope Mrs. Byrd is nice," Patti said.

Gilbert stopped walking and said, "Uh-oh. What if she's not?"

Patti pulled his arm. "Then we'd better walk fast. If we're late, maybe she'll send us to the principal!"

"He looks mean," Gilbert said. "Let's walk very, very fast."

When they got to school, Patti's mother introduced them. The very tall teacher bent down. "Hello, Patti. Hello, Gilbert," she said, smiling. "Please leave your things in your cubbies. Then go sit on the carpet."

Patti hugged her mother good-bye. Gilbert wished that his mother was there to hug, too.

Gilbert found a cubbyhole with his name and his photograph on it. He looked at the photographs on the other cubbies. He didn't know anyone except Patti.

Patti sat down next to a girl named Margaret, and Gilbert sat next to Patti. Patti talked and laughed with Margaret until Mrs. Byrd turned the lights off and on. Their kindergarten teacher never turned the lights off and on. Everyone suddenly grew quiet.

"Good morning and welcome to first grade," Mrs. Byrd said.

A boy named Philip held up a big fat book and said, "I know how to read."

Mrs. Byrd smiled and said, "Thank you for sharing, Philip. This year we will all learn how to read. Now, everyone, please take your seats."

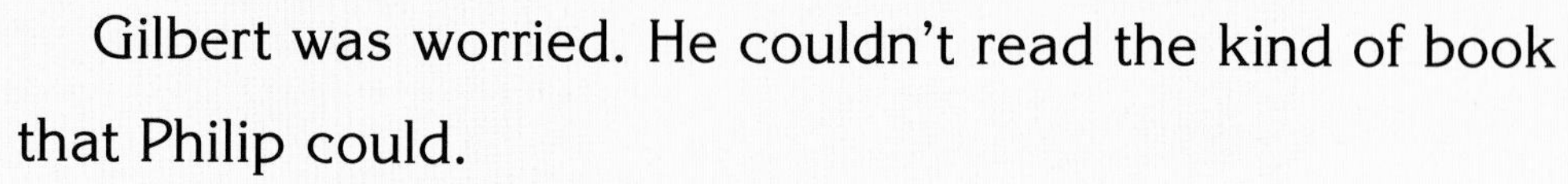

Gilbert was worried. He couldn't read the kind of book that Philip could.

Gilbert took the desk next to Patti's. Suddenly a big kid said, "Can't you read?" He pointed to the name taped to the front of the desk. "It says L-E-W-I-S. That spells Lewis."

Gilbert turned red. He didn't know there were names on the desks! He quickly got up and found a desk that said G-I-L-B-E-R-T. A boy was already sitting there. The boy turned red and moved to the desk that said F-R-A-N-K.

Mrs. Byrd handed out spelling books and reading books and special paper to write on. Gilbert could see that first grade was going to be hard!

At snack time, Lewis shouted, "Oh boy—chocolate cookies!"

Mrs. Byrd turned to him and said, "We don't shout in class, Lewis. That's a rule in first grade." She wrote on the chalkboard, *Rules: 1. Use your quiet voice.* Then she asked, "What are some other rules we should follow?"

Patti raised her hand and said, "We should say *please* and *thank you.*" Mrs. Byrd wrote it on the board. Gilbert knew that rule and wished he had said it first.

Mrs. Byrd listed all the rules they could think of, until Gilbert finally added, "You should always sit at the right desk!"

RULES:
1. Use your quiet voice.
2. Say "please" and "thank you."
3. Keep your desk tidy.
4. Cover your mouth when you sneeze.
5. Do not pick yo
6. Do not pus

At lunchtime, Mrs. Byrd brought her class to the cafeteria. Gilbert had never eaten in the cafeteria with the big kids before. He looked for Patti, but she was already sitting next to Margaret.

There was an empty seat next to Lewis, but Gilbert didn't want to sit there. He finally sat by himself.

He wasn't hungry, but if he didn't eat his lunch, maybe he would get sent to the principal!

As he started eating, Mrs. Byrd walked toward him. "Oh, here's a seat," she said to the boy named Frank. Frank sat down next to Gilbert, and Gilbert saw that he had the exact same Martian Space Pilot lunchbox.

At recess, Frank and Gilbert climbed all the way to the top of the climbing fort. Philip was a good reader, but he was not a good climber. When he tried to go up the ladder, he kept tripping on his big feet.

After recess, they painted pictures to go into the rule book.

Lewis was a good climber, but he was not a very good painter. He spilled green paint all over his desk. He yelled, "AARRGGHH!," forgetting all about rule number one, not to shout in class.

After they cleaned up, it was quiet time. Gilbert thought that quiet time meant nap time, like in kindergarten, but it really meant that everyone could pick out a book to read alone.

Gilbert picked a Frog and Toad book and brought it to the beanbag chair. Everyone was very quiet. Especially Lewis. He had fallen asleep, reading *Goodnight Moon*!

Margaret

When the bell rang at the end of the day, Gilbert wasn't ready to go home. He was still reading *Frog and Toad Are Friends* when his mother came to pick him up. Philip was helping him with the words he didn't know.

"I know how to read," Gilbert announced proudly.

“Take the book home, Gilbert,” Mrs. Byrd said. “See if you can finish it.”

“I have homework, too,” Lola said to Mrs. Byrd. “I have to write my name ten times. School is very hard.”

On the way home, Patti and Gilbert agreed that Mrs. Byrd was very nice.

Then Gilbert asked his sister, “Did you like Mrs. Duck, Lola?”

“Yes,” said Lola. “And I like my new friend. His name is Sam.”

"I made a new friend, too," Gilbert said. "And so did Patti."

Patti said, "No, I didn't. Margaret is my friend from dance class. She's an old friend. Just like you, Gilbert."

"Oh," Gilbert said. He was glad that he was still Patti's old friend.

When they got home, Lola got a pencil and paper. She wrote her name ten times.

"I can read," she said to Gilbert. Then she read, "Lola, Lola, Lola, Lola, Lola, Lola, Lola, Lola, Lola, Lola."

"I can read, too," Gilbert said. He read *Frog and Toad Are Friends* to Lola. He guessed at the words that he didn't know, but Lola said he was a good reader, just like Mrs. Duck.

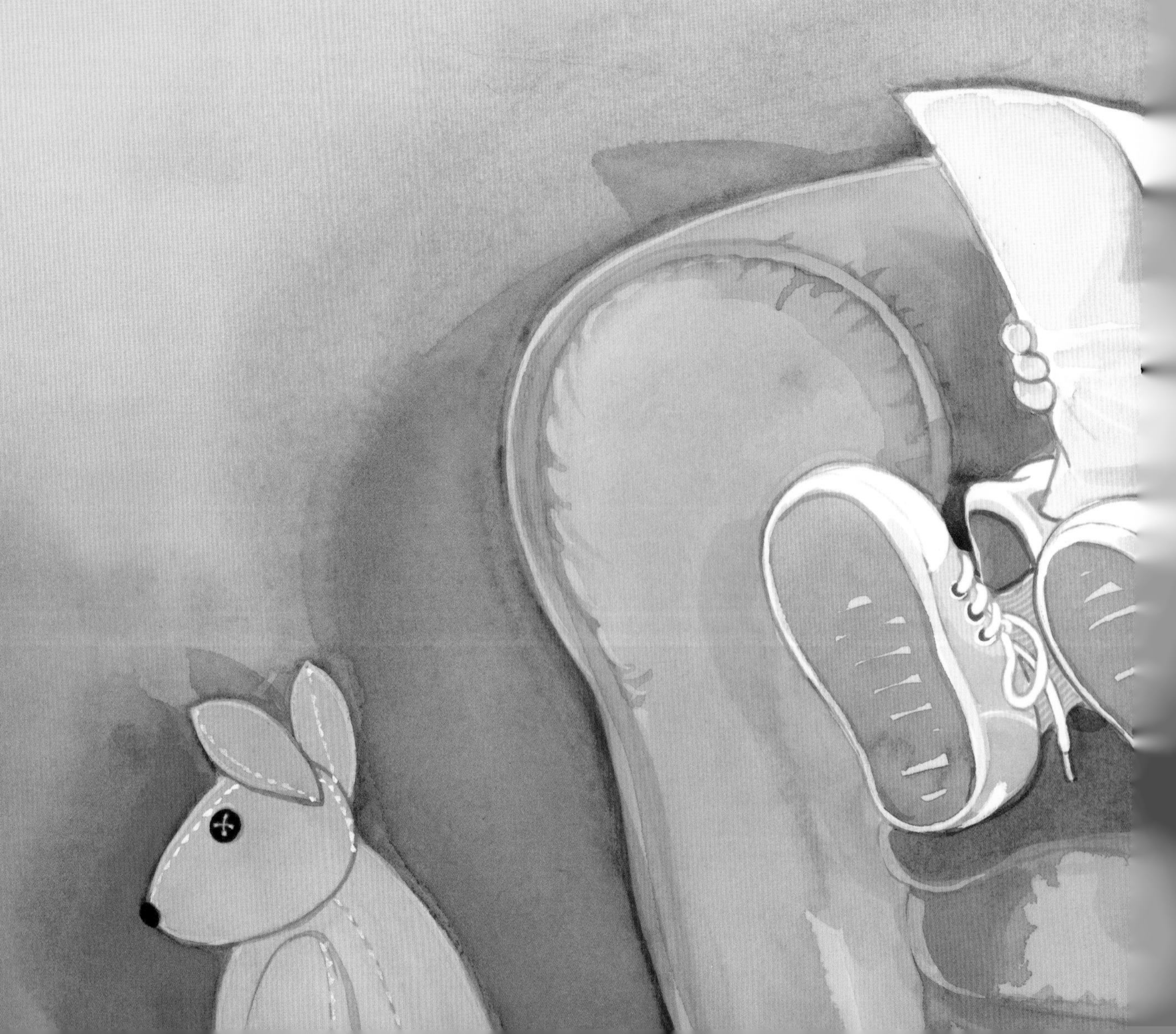

After dinner, they went out for ice cream to celebrate the first day of school. When they walked into the ice cream shop, Gilbert said, “Look, there’s my friend Frank!”

Lola said, “There’s my friend Sam!”

Father said, “And there’s Mr. Pug, the principal!”

Lola and Sam ate strawberry ice cream, and Gilbert and Frank ate chocolate. Mr. Pug had pistachio ice cream with sprinkles on top.

And Gilbert knew that, as a rule, anyone who liked sprinkles on their ice cream had to be a very nice person!